Economically Developing Countries

India

David Cumming

Thomson Learning
New York

Economically Developing Countries

Bangladesh　　　**Egypt**
Brazil　　　　　**Ghana**
China　　　　　**India**

Cover: Hindu worshipers wait to bathe in the Ganges.
Title page: A busy street in central Jaipur
Contents page: Desert people in Rajasthan travel into town to do their shopping.

Picture acknowledgments: The publisher would like to thank the following for allowing their photographs to be reproduced in this book:
Actionaid (Liba Taylor) 39, 40, 41; Actionaid 42, 43; Camera Press 9 (Dinodia), 15 (top and bottom), 35; David Cumming *title page*, 3, 4 (top), 6, 10, 11, 14, 17, 18, 19, 20, 21, 23, 24, 25, 26, 27, 28, 31, 32, 34, 36, 38, 44, 45; Eye Ubiquitous 8 (Martin Reeves), 16 (David Cumming), 33 (Jason Burke), 37 (C. Johnson); (Chris Gibb) 7; Peter Newark's Historical Pictures 13; Zul, Chapel Studios 22, 29.
Photographs on pages 4 (bottom), 12, and 30 come from the Wayland Picture Library. All artwork by Peter Bull.

First published in the
United States in 1995 by
Thomson Learning
New York, NY

First published in Great Britain in 1995 by
Wayland (Publishers) Ltd.

Library of Congress Cataloging-in-Publication Data

Cumming, David, 1953–
  India / David Cumming.
      p.   cm. —(Economically developing countries)
  Includes bibliographical references and index.
  Summary: Describes India's physical environment and the effects of colonialism before going on to discuss the current social and economic situations and a possible future.
  ISBN 1-56847-384-2 (hc)
  1. India—Economic conditions—1947–   —Juvenile literature.
2. India—Social conditions—1947–   —Juvenile literature. 3. Economic forecasting—India—Juvenile literature. [1. India.]
I. Title. II. Series.
HC435.2.C85   1995
330.945—dc20   95-19622

Printed in Italy

Contents

India Today

India occupies the huge triangle of land poking out of the continent of Asia into the Indian Ocean. It is bordered by six nations: Pakistan, China, Nepal, Bhutan, Bangladesh, and Myanmar (previously Burma). Two of its neighbors, Pakistan and Bangladesh, used to be part of India until the country was divided in 1947. India is above the equator, which means it is in the Northern Hemisphere.

India has nearly 17 percent of all the people in the world. Or, to put it another way, every sixth person in the world is an Indian. Hindi and Bengali, two of India's major languages, are the fifth and sixth most-spoken languages in the world. With a population of over 900 million, only China has more people.

India is a confusing country. Its scientists and computer experts are among the best, capable of producing the most modern technology and of successfully rocketing satellites into space. So it would seem to be a modern, industrialized nation. Yet in no other country do so many people work on the land and live in extreme poverty. For these reasons, India is still considered to be a developing nation.

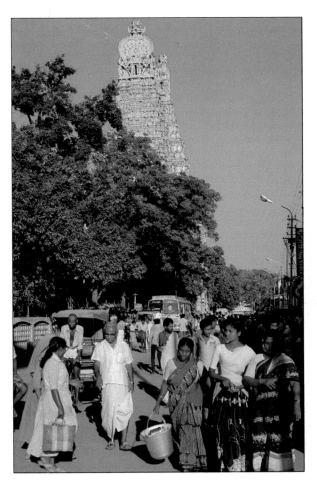

India has 36 cities that are each home to more than 500,000 people. However, the majority of Indian people live in the country, where facilities such as education and health care are limited.

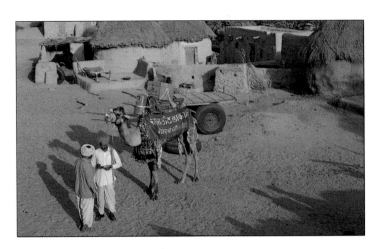

In the desert state of Rajasthan, camels are an important means of transportation, used even for delivering the mail.

INDIA AT A GLANCE

Land area	1,269,219 square miles
Main cities (population in millions)	Bombay (9.9), New Delhi (9.5), Calcutta (4.4)
Population	931 million (estimate for 1995)
Currency	Rupee, divided into 100 paise
Main languages	Hindi and English, plus 15 regional languages
Longest rivers	Brahmaputra (1,800 miles); Ganges (1,559 miles)
Highest points	K-2 (28,250 feet) and Kangchenjunga (28,208 feet)

India has an enormous variety of country including hot, humid jungles in the south, desert in the northwest, and the snow-capped Himalayas in the northeast, on the border with China.

India has not always been like this. It had been a prosperous country, but internal conflicts left India susceptible to invasion and eventual takeover by the British in the 1700s. In 1947, the British gave India its independence, but India by then had become a poor, backward country. Getting India back on its feet has not been easy. Putting right the wrongs of history has been delayed by nature and by Indian society itself.

5

The Physical Environment

India is the seventh largest country in the world: roughly 2,000 miles from north to south, and 1,700 miles across at its widest point. It is one-third the size of the United States including Alaska and Hawaii, and occupies most of the Indian subcontinent of southern Asia.

FARMLAND

Poor soils and a lack of water mean that only 55 percent of India is fit for farming. Deforestation and overgrazing on much of the land have led to the erosion, by wind and rain, of topsoil from the northern highlands and the Deccan plateau. Fertilizers have to be used to encourage plant growth in the thin, stony soil that remains.

The best soil lies on the plains between the Himalayas and the Deccan, across which the Ganges River meanders to the Bay of Bengal. This soil is formed of a deep layer of alluvium, dropped over the centuries by the Ganges and its many tributaries when they flood. The alluvium is good for farming because it is rich in the nutrients that crops, such as rice, wheat, and vegetables, need for good growth.

The most fertile land lies in the river valleys. Here, in the northern state of Ladakh, water from the Indus River is used to irrigate farming land.

THE IMPORTANCE OF THE MONSOON

No matter how good the soil, nothing will grow in it unless it is well watered. The farmers on the Ganges plains are fortunate because plenty of water is available from the river, via irrigation channels and from under the ground. The rest of India's farmers have to rely on the monsoon for rain.

India has three seasons:

• Winter (lasting from October to February) is mostly warm and dry. Although temperatures plunge well below freezing point in the Himalayas, they average 80°F in the south.

• Spring (March to May) is hot and dry.

• Summer (June to September) is wet and very hot, with temperatures soaring to 110°F.

The rain is brought by the monsoon, a wind from the southwest. Blowing in from the equator, it picks up moisture over the Indian Ocean. The monsoon soaks the south first, usually around the end of May. Then, at a steady 12 miles per hour, it moves across the whole country, reaching the northwest by the middle of July.

The monsoon is both a help and a hindrance. Some years it brings so much rain that there are destructive floods in much of India.

CLIMATE

New Delhi			Madras		
Month	Average temp (°F)	Average rainfall (in)	Month	Average temp (°F)	Average rainfall (in)
Jan	57	0.90	Jan	75	1.4
Feb	63	0.70	Feb	77	0.39
March	73	0.51	March	82	0.31
April	82	0.31	April	88	0.59
May	93	0.51	May	91	0.98
June	93	2.9	June	91	1.89
July	90	7.0	July	88	3.5
Aug	86	6.7	Aug	88	4.6
Sept	84	4.6	Sept	86	4.68
Oct	79	0.39	Oct	82	13.3
Nov	84	0.12	Nov	79	14
Dec	61	0.39	Dec	77	5.5

The monsoon is a mischievous wind, which does both harm and good. Some years it arrives early and catches everyone by surprise with a lot of rain. Floods can drown people and animals, wash away land and property, and generally cause chaos. In September 1980, heavy monsoon rains caused the Ganges River to burst its banks: 1,600 people died, 43,000 villages were flooded, and the city of Calcutta was knee-deep in water. In other years, the monsoon will arrive late and drop hardly any rain. Cattle die of thirst, farmers' fields dry up, and people are threatened by food shortages. In between these extremes, there are years when the monsoon brings enough rain for good harvests.

Though it is troublesome, the monsoon is vital to millions of India's farmers. Although it blows for only a few months in the summer, the monsoon brings 70 percent of all the rain falling on India every year. There is little rain during winter or spring, which means that some areas are dry for eight months of the year. Unless farmers can irrigate their fields during this time, they cannot grow any crops.

Length of Dry Season	Length of Wet Season
9 months or more dry	3 months or less wet
7-8 months dry	4-5 months wet
5-6 months dry	6-7 months wet
3-4 months dry	8-9 months wet
2 months or less dry	10 months or more wet
Growth interrupted by period of frost	

Although the amount of rainfall varies from region to region, it all falls during the monsoon season.

A waterwheel, powered by cows, raises water from an irrigation ditch into a field.

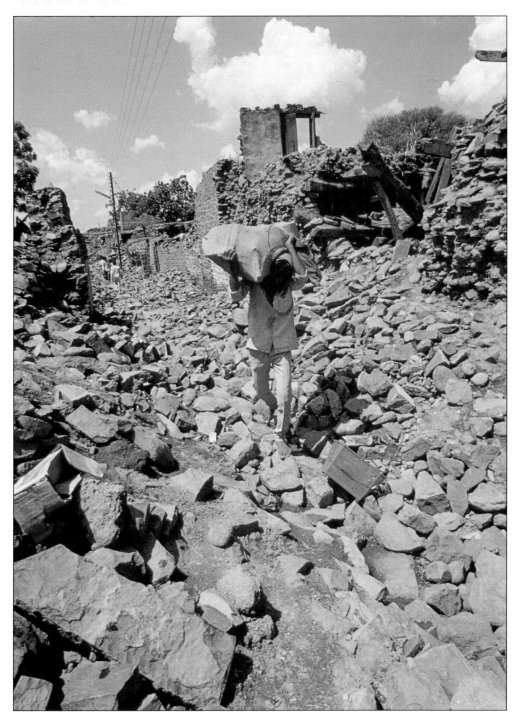

Only 20 percent of the farmland is irrigated, which means that 80 percent of Indian farmers rely on the monsoon. They sow their seeds in the spring and harvest their crops when the rains have stopped. They can grow little food until the following summer, when the monsoon will again provide water for their crops.

Earthquakes are also natural hindrances to India's progress. This man is clearing debris after the 1993 earthquake in Maharashtra.

DESTRUCTIVE EARTHQUAKES

Life in India is also disrupted by earthquakes, which are common. On September 30, 1993, an earthquake lasting only seconds shook 200 square miles of Maharashtra state. The official death toll was 9,748, although some sources reported 30,000 deaths. It will cost about $90 million to repair the damage to structures and other property.

The Effects of Colonialism

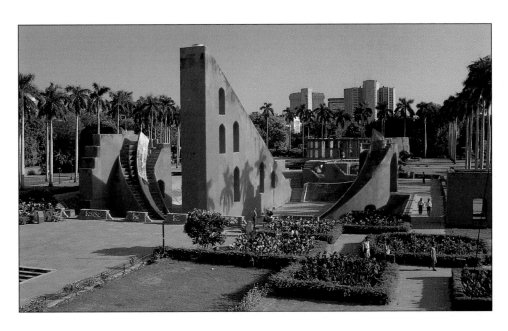

Built in 1725, the Jantar Mantar observatory in New Delhi was used to revise the calendar and to check on ancient astronomical calculations.

Most people think that India benefited from the arrival of Europeans, that they, with their supposedly more advanced ways, generously modernized a backward nation to help the people living there. In fact, the reverse is nearer the truth, since there is much evidence to show that the Europeans did more harm than good to India. Instead of offering India a helping hand, the Europeans, particularly the British, deliberately held back India's progress.

Europeans came to India in the 1500s to trade and to learn, for in many areas India was ahead of the rest of the world. European astronomers found that their Indian counterparts were using accurate tables for their calculations that had been compiled in 3100 B.C. They also discovered that Aryabhata, an astronomer working in A.D. 500, knew that the earth was round and that a year lasted 365.3586 days. In 1790, Professor John Playfair of Edinburgh University, Scotland, concluded that astronomical observations were being made in India "when all Europe was barbarous."

Indian mathematicians provided the world with the concept of zero as a number, the decimal system, and a method of multiplication used in calculating machines before modern-day computers were invented. They were also working with many algebraic and geometrical formulas well before mathematicians in Europe.

In 325 B.C. steel, called *wootz*, started to be made in India, long before it was made anywhere else. The production of *wootz* was complicated, one of the processes requiring temperatures of 2,300°F. A sample of *wootz* was sent to London in the 1700s, where a scientist at the Royal Society said it was "decidedly the best [steel] I have yet met with." In 1842 British metallurgists praised the quality of Indian iron. Later, they were astounded to learn that it was made more efficiently and cheaply than in Great Britain, where new factories were thought to be the best in the world. A 23-foot tall *wootz* pillar in the Qutab Minar courtyard in Delhi does not have a speck of rust on it, despite having been in the open air since A.D. 500. The reason it is rust free is still a mystery.

Indian society, too, was well organized when the Europeans arrived. The farmers grew sufficient food throughout the year for everyone to be well fed. Their methods were a model of environmental friendliness. Doctors, using centuries-old remedies based on natural, medicinal herbs, kept sickness away. They knew about vaccination long before European doctors.

There was a good education system, with schools within reach of every village. Indeed, when the Europeans arrived, there were probably more literate people in India than in Europe. The arts and three major religions—Hinduism, Islam, and Buddhism—flourished. India was far from being a backward country. If anything, the Europeans needed the help of India.

The Qutab Minar's iron pillar is about 1,600 years old. It continues to amaze people because it is free of rust, despite having been in the open air all the time.

THE EAST INDIA COMPANY

On December 31, 1600, the British government gave the East India Company permission to be the only British firm to trade with India. From then on, the company was in charge of selling British goods in India and Indian goods in Great Britain. It could keep everything it earned from this business. The company's owners were delighted: India was theirs, and they could do whatever they liked with it. All they wanted to do with India was to make money from it—lots of money. For nearly 300 years the company saw India as a bottomless treasure chest which it could plunder.

The East India Company opened offices and factories in India, which it protected with its own army. Soon the soldiers were being used to conquer Indian rulers who were reluctant to trade with the company. Their lands were then taken over by the company. Eventually, the company was governing much of India. The British considered themselves superior to the Indians and showed them no respect, often treating them poorly. The company encouraged its staff to earn as much as possible, irrespective of the suffering they caused.

British Territory by 1805

Protected states

British Territory after 1856

KASHMIR

PUNJAB

RAJPUT LANDS

BENGAL

Calcutta

Bombay

Madras

The British did not directly control all of India, but their influence extended over the entire country until 1947.

There were rebellions against British rule in India, notably the Sepoy Mutiny of 1857-58, but such rebellions were crushed. This drawing shows some rebels being executed by hanging and by being fired out of gun barrels.

DESTRUCTION OF FARMLAND

The East India Company introduced a high land tax, forcing farmers to pay 50 percent of their earnings. "The idea," as a company manager admitted, "is to get as much as possible out of the *ryot* [peasant farmer] and when no more is to be got out of him, let him go to the Devil!" Many farmers could not pay the taxes, so they sold their property to wealthy landowners, called *zamindars*. The *zamindars* allowed the farmers to remain on their land in return for paying them rent. Farmers who could not afford the rent were thrown off their land. If they were not replaced, the land went to waste. As a result, about 30 percent of good farming land became useless, and food production fell.

The East India Company also reduced the amount of food grown by forcing farmers to plant cash crops, such as cotton, indigo, tea, and jute, which were for selling, not for eating. Previously, enough food had been grown for some to be stored for the years when there was no rain. Now, there was no surplus food to put aside, so there were famines when the monsoon failed. The worst was in 1777, when 10 million people died in Bengal.

The company cut down many of India's forests to make ships and railroad ties and so the land could be used for coffee and tea plantations. To ensure there would be enough timber for its needs, the company made laws to keep Indians out of the forests and introduced a firewood tax. Consequently, cattle dung replaced wood as a cooking fuel. There was less dung to fertilize the soil, so much good farming soil lost its nutrients, and food production declined even further.

One of the worst famines in India's history was in the northern state of Bihar in 1770, where 30 percent of the people died.

The skilled craftsmanship needed to build and to decorate this southern Indian temple shows how advanced India was when the British arrived.

EDUCATION

The East India Company's land reforms also affected the education system. Most schools had been self-financing. They had been given their own land, which they used to grow food for their staff and pupils, as well as a source of income to pay their running costs. The new land tax made this impossible, and many schools had to shut.

All the money raised by taxes went back to Great Britain. Before these taxes were introduced, this money would have stayed in India. India's raw materials, such as cotton, were also taken back to Great Britain. The East India Company did not develop any industries in India, for fear that they would compete with the factories in Great Britain. Little was invested in India unless it was absolutely necessary. Much was spent on building railroads, but only because they helped the British to get goods to and from the harbors.

In 1784, members of the British Parliament, appalled by what had been going on in India, forced the government to shut the East India Company and to take over the running of India itself. By then it was too late: India had been crippled. Before the British arrived, India had been prosperous and self-sufficient. Now, the majority of its people were landless, ill fed, illiterate, and poor. Farmland had been ruined and industries were undeveloped.

We did not conquer India for the benefit of the Indians. We conquered India as the outlet of goods of Great Britain.
—Lord Brentford, speaking in 1931

14

INDEPENDENCE FROM BRITISH RULE

By the late 1800s, the seeds of dissatisfaction had been sown in India. An independence movement grew and gathered momentum in the 1920s, under the leadership of Mahatma Gandhi. His demands for the British to "quit India" and to give Indians *swaraj*, or self-rule, were finally answered in 1947, when India became an independent country.

The British may have left nearly 50 years ago, but India still has not recovered from their rule. It will take a long time for the scars of colonialism to heal.

By the 1930s, many Indians supported Gandhi in trying to force the British out of India. Here, police break up an anti-British demonstration in Calcutta.

You have been taught that … British rule in India is beneficial. Nothing is more false! You cannot escape two facts: first, that under the British, India has become the world's poorest country; and second, that it is denied advantages and decencies to which any free country is entitled.
—**Mahatma Gandhi**

MOHANDAS GANDHI (1869–1948)

Born in India, Gandhi studied in Great Britain before working as a lawyer in South Africa, where he helped to make the government repeal laws that were unjust to Indians. After returning to India, his peaceful protests against British rule encouraged rural people to follow his example and eventually force the British to leave. He was known as the *Mahatma*, or "great soul," because his simple, honest lifestyle inspired Indians to rebel against their colonial rulers by non-violent protest.

To millions of Indians, Mahatma Gandhi was just like them: he dressed and lived very simply. They followed him without question.

15

Measuring Development

People often talk about the world's rich and poor countries. Poor countries are often referred to as developing, while rich ones are developed.

There are many different ways of measuring how developed a country is. One way is to look at how much wealth a country produces, or its gross national product per person (or GNP per capita). This is the wealth created each year by its industries within its borders, plus the money earned from exports, divided by the country's population. The GNP per capita is the amount of money each person in a country would receive if all the wealth was shared equally. Obviously, the bigger a country's GNP, the larger each person's share would be. Rich countries would be able to give their people a lot of money, while poor countries would give theirs a small amount.

The wealth in any country is not shared equally. In India, few people are rich, and many, such as this rickshaw puller, are poor.

GROSS NATIONAL PRODUCT PER CAPITA ($)		
Rank	GNP per capita	
1	Switzerland	36,080
6	United States	23,240
13	Canada	20,710
16	Great Britain	17,790
17	Australia	17,260
22	New Zealand	12,300
105	China	470
115	India	310
123	Bangladesh	220
132	Mozambique	60

Source: *World Development Report*, World Bank, 1994

Poverty is obvious in much of India. Beggars in cities like Calcutta are often desperate for food.

Switzerland has the highest GNP per person, whereas India ranks 115th out of 132 countries. Switzerland is the richest country in the world and India is the eighteenth poorest.

However, a single number such as GNP per capita can be misleading. No country in the world divides its wealth equally among all of its people. There are other ways of determining which are developed and which are developing countries.

According to some experts, for a country to be considered developed:

• there should be no poverty; its people should have the basic necessities of life: food, shelter, clothing, health care, and education.

• there should be no unemployment; its people should have jobs to earn money for buying the things they need and also for their self-respect—to feel that they are contributing something to society.

• there should be no inequality; everyone should be treated justly and fairly, regardless of their backgrounds, wealth, or gender.

No country can completely wipe out poverty, unemployment, and inequality. However, in a developed country these exist on a smaller scale than in a developing nation, where there are many poor people, high unemployment, and great inequalities. Like any developing nation, India has its share of these three problems.

17

Even the children who go to school are poorly educated because their schools lack basic facilities such as classrooms, desks, and textbooks.

POVERTY IN INDIA

India has some of the poorest people in the world, and not just a few million, but hundreds of millions of them. It has been estimated that as much as 48 percent of India's population (406 million people) are poor. (In the United States in 1992, 14.5 percent of the population, or 36.9 million people, were considered poor.)

These people's poverty can be measured by the extent to which they are denied many of the basic necessities of daily life, such as clean drinking water, health care, and education: the less a person has of these, the poorer he tends to be.

Providing the poor with more basic necessities would give them opportunities to be better off, not only in terms of having more money, but in having a better life. Not having life's basic necessities is poverty.

For some people, it is difficult even to earn enough money to buy food.

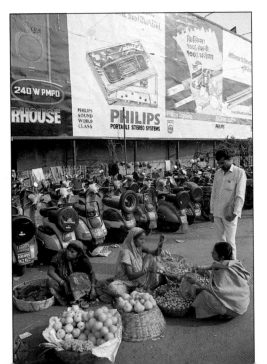

WHO IS POOR IN INDIA?

In the Indian government's eyes, you are rich or poor according to whether you can afford to buy enough food for your minimum daily energy requirements. Poor people cannot afford the minimum number of calories, while rich people can. The government says that rural people need to eat a minimum of 2,400 calories and city people 2,100 calories each day. (Country life is tougher, so rural people need more energy.)

- 63 percent of Indian children under 5 years old are malnourished; Bangladesh is the only country in the world where the problem is worse.*
- An Indian woman can expect to live to 62, a man to 61, an American woman to 80 and a man to 73.*
- India has one doctor for 2,460 people; the United States has one doctor for 420 people.*
- In India, there are 1,000 people per hospital bed; in Great Britain there are 200.**
- 14 percent of India's population has access to sanitation and 73 percent to safe water; in most Western countries, everyone has access to sanitation and safe water.*
- 52 percent of Indian adults cannot read and write; in European countries it is less than 5 percent.*
- In India there is one teacher for every 60 primary school children; in Canada there is one teacher for 15 children.*

Source: * *World Development Report*, World Bank, 1994
** *World Development Report*, 1990

It is difficult for the poor to break out of their poverty. The areas where they live have bad facilities, which means that they have very limited opportunities to better themselves. For example, because there are few schools people cannot get decent educations, which means that they cannot get jobs that pay well, so they are not able to improve their lives.

Unable to satisfy the basic needs of nearly half its population, India itself is a developing country. It cannot begin to think of itself as a developed nation until this level of poverty has been greatly reduced.

With no running water in their homes, these men are forced to wash on the street.

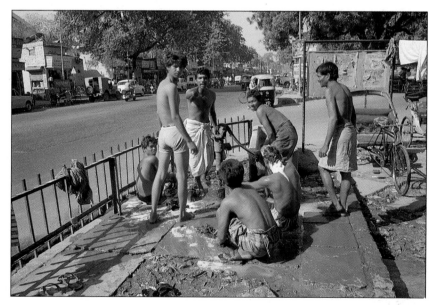

Working in India

India does not have enough jobs for all its population. There are a large number of people who are either unemployed or underemployed. The unemployed have no jobs whatsoever. Underemployed people have no regular full-time jobs. Instead, they do odd jobs, perhaps working only for a few hours a week or for one or two days per week or month.

No one is sure how many people are unemployed in India. However, after carrying out the population census in 1991, the government estimated it to be 36 million people, or 12.5 percent of the total workforce.

DISTRIBUTION OF THE WORKFORCE		
	India	U.S.
Agriculture	62%	2%
Manufacturing industries	11%	24%
Service industries	27%	74%
Source: *World Development Report*, World Bank, 1990		

Many Indians earn some money from part-time work because there are not enough jobs for everyone to work all the time.

There are probably the same number of underemployed people. If so, this means that about 72 million people, or 25 percent of the workforce, are not receiving adequate wages. Assuming that these people have three dependants to support, then a total of 270 million or so persons' lives are affected by a lack of money, more than the entire population of the United States.

As countries develop, it is usual for people to stop working on the land and to find jobs in factories. In India, more people still work on the land than in industries because there are not enough factory jobs. The reasons for this are partly historical and partly connected with population growth.

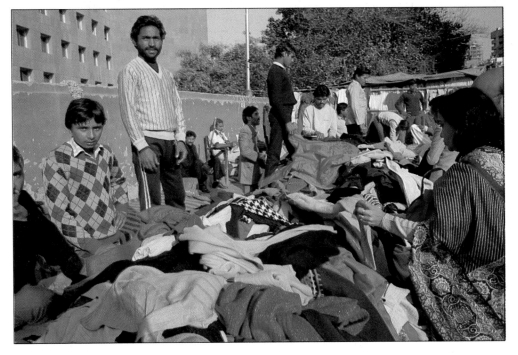

FEW FACTORIES

India has few factories, because its industrialization started only after independence. The British had used India as a source of cheap, agricultural raw materials. Instead of turning India into a nation of factory workers, the British kept it a nation of farmers. The only factories built in India were for processing crops for shipping back to Great Britain. Jute and cotton mills, for example, were constructed to prepare the raw farm crops for the factories at home. Independence from Great Britain gave India the freedom to start industrializing.

In 1947, industries employed less than 10 percent of the workforce. Today, they still employ only 11 percent of the total number of workers.

Most of India's industries are located near the coast, to be close to shipping ports.

N

New Delhi

Calcutta

Bombay

Goa

Bangalore

Madras

○ Steel plant
▼ Oil and gas
▲ Oil refineries
■ Major port
◆ Major iron ore mine
✶ Petrochemical plant
▽ Space center
◇ Shipyard
□ Nuclear power station
△ Aircraft manufacture
┼┼┼┼ Railroad

TOO MANY WORKERS

The other reason for India's high unemployment and underemployment is population growth. Although industries have been built quickly, the population has grown even faster. Every day, 70,000 babies are born in India—nearly one per second—and the population has been growing by two percent per year, or over 19 million people. (In comparison, the population of the U.S. increases by 0.9 percent per year.)

I didn't want seven children; my husband did. He wanted to impress his friends. He also thought the children would make him rich, but they've only made us poorer. It's so expensive now to educate, feed, and clothe them that I've told my eldest daughter to stop at two children, no matter what her husband says.
—Tulika Kapoor, a mother from Delhi

In India, there are more small workshops, like this one in Calcutta, than factories.

THE IMPORTANCE OF AGRICULTURE

As there are few factories, city jobs are scarce. Most people who go in search of them are disappointed. They end up doing odd jobs and increasing the number of underemployed. The other alternative is to remain in the countryside to work on the land. Agriculture employs 62 percent of all workers.

A minority make a good living from the land. They are people with large farms in good areas—mainly on the Ganges plain—where they can grow enough for their own needs and still have a lot of surplus crops to sell for an income.

However, the majority of people in agriculture are either subsistence farmers or laborers, both of whom scratch a living from the land. The subsistence farmers can grow enough to feed themselves, but little or nothing is left over to sell. Many of them farm in areas where the soil is poor and where there is no irrigation during the dry season. They do not have the money to improve their land and have to do the best they can with their limited resources.

A farmer's wife drying coriander seeds. She is fortunate in having enough land so that some crops can be sold for an income.

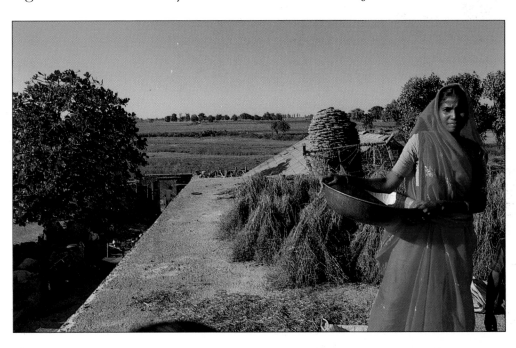

THE GREEN REVOLUTION—SUCCESS OR FAILURE?

The Green Revolution is the name given to the changes in agriculture in the last 20 years. The most important one was the introduction of new types of wheat and rice, called high-yielding varieties (HYVs), which increased the size of harvests. However, HYVs required a lot of fertilizers, pesticides, and regular watering. Rich farmers could afford to plant HYVs: they had the money to buy the fertilizers and the pesticides and improve their irrigation systems. Poor farmers had to borrow money, which increased their debts. Often, they have not been able to keep on buying the fertilizers and chemicals, so their HYV crops have failed. In much of India, the Green Revolution has only made rich farmers richer and poor farmers even poorer.

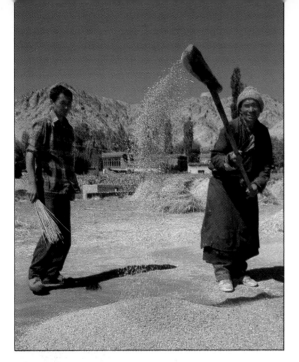

Winnowing the wheat harvest in Ladakh. The soil there is frozen for several months during the cold winters, so nothing can be grown in it and farmers have no work.

Agricultural laborers earn their money from working for farmers, perhaps by helping them to gather the harvest or to sow seeds. Most of their work is seasonal and dependent on the weather. If the monsoon fails or washes away the crops, they get no work. Most agricultural laborers are underemployed.

The 1991 census estimated that 6 percent of all agricultural male workers were unemployed. However, when the numbers of underemployed were included, this rose to 23 percent. In 1991, 191 million worked in agriculture, so about 44 million men did not earn full wages. And this figure does not include women workers.

Even if they had been in full-time work they would have earned little. India's population boom has been most noticeable in the countryside, for this is where the majority of the people live. While the number of rural workers has increased, the amount of land, and therefore the number of jobs, has remained the same. As there are more people wanting work than there are jobs available, wages are low.

Rice, wheat, and corn are the main Indian crops.

N

Rice

Forest

Highland pasture

Unproductive land

Arable wheat and corn

MONEY FROM FARMING

Each year, the amount of money India earns from agriculture gets smaller. This shrinking sum has to be shared by more and more people, which means that farmers and agricultural laborers are worse off. In fact, recent studies show that they are earning the same amount of money as they did in the 1950s, although the cost of living today is much higher.

23

This Delhi teenager has probably been working for ten years already, to boost his family's income.

For the majority of families, income is more important than education. Many children start working as soon as they can walk and talk.

CHILD LABOR

The high numbers of unemployed and underemployed adults have caused an increase in the number of children who work. With their fathers earning little or nothing, the children are used to add to the family income.

There are few job opportunities in their villages, so the children are sent to the nearest towns or cities where they do anything offered to them: from sidewalk shoe shining and running errands in hotels to jobs in factories or workshops.

Except for the fact that child labor is widespread, no one knows how many children work. However, it seems safe to assume that if an adult replaced every child worker, there would be little unemployment or underemployment in India, and millions would be better off.

I never went to school, so I cannot read or write. I've been working for as long as I can remember. I sell snacks to the people on the Maidan, the huge park in the center of Calcutta.
—Arun, age 13

24

Most employers "buy" children from parents desperate for money. The employers look upon the children as their slaves, treating them badly, paying them little, and making them work long hours in unhealthy conditions. Many children start working at a young age. For example, a recent study of the carpet industry found that 300,000 children were employed in it, 18 percent (54,000) of whom were under ten years old.

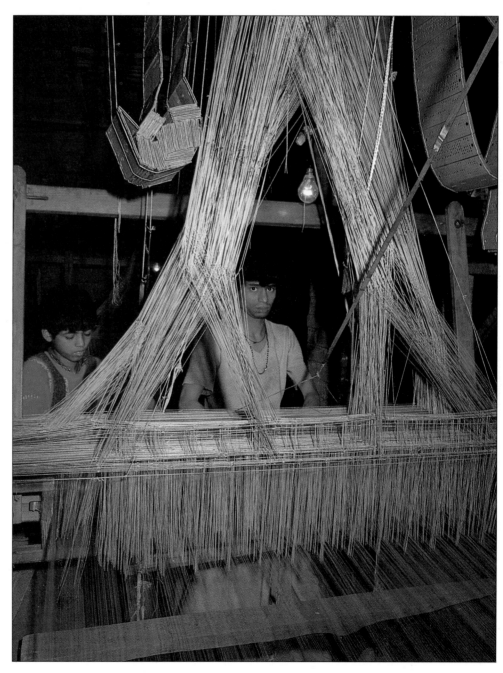

A silk-weaving workshop. Most of the workers in this industry are children, who work in poor conditions for little money.

Street children of Bangalore

Bangalore is the capital of the southern state of Karnataka. It is one of the biggest cities in India, with a population of 3.3 million. Bangalore is the "Silicon City" of India, full of booming computer and electronics businesses. Space satellites are also made there and launched nearby. These new industries have made Bangalore one of the richest cities in India. Despite this, more than 40 percent of its population lives in slums. Unable to make ends meet, many families have been forced to send their children out to work. Most of them end up on the streets. Here, they are joined by the children who have left home because of family problems brought on by the stresses of slum life and poverty.

There are 45,000 children living and working on Bangalore's streets. About 25,000 of them stay on the streets the whole time, both day and night. Some are orphans with no family to support them. Others have left home because they were unhappy there. Some of these children keep in contact with their parents, while others want nothing to do with them. The remaining 20,000 children work on the streets in the day and return home in the evening with what they have earned.

One of Bangalore's many homeless children keeps warm at night, before curling up to sleep somewhere on the street.

The children who have to go out to earn money work in dark, dusty conditions. They develop bad eyesight and breathing problems, which will stop them from working. When they become adults, they may be forced to send their

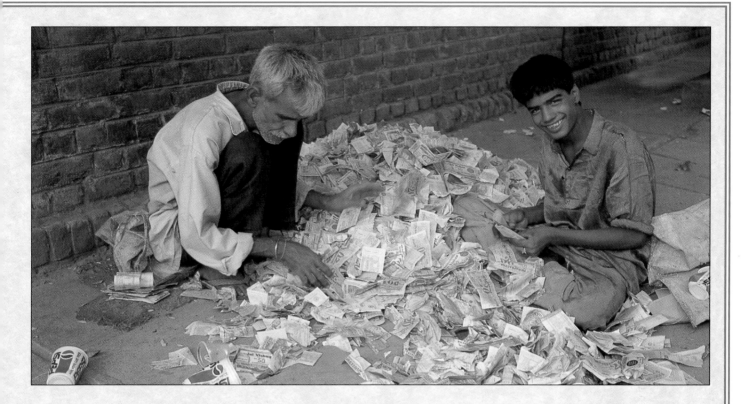

Sorting used lottery tickets before taking them to a recycler, who will sell them to a paper mill

The ages of the street children range from five or six to late teenagers. About 60 percent of them are rag pickers, who rummage through garbage for waste, such as paper, plastic, or cardboard, for recyclers. In return, the recyclers pay them a few rupees per pound or give them food and shelter.

Living on the streets brings the children into contact with the criminals of Bangalore. They often tempt the children into theft, prostitution, or dealing in drugs. The children are constantly harassed by the police and they are sometimes kidnaped by "slum agents," who force them to work as virtual slaves in factories or hotels.

My parents live in Bangalore. They are drunkards. They used to hit me and shout at me every day. In the end I left home and went to live on the streets. That was six years ago.
—Padmanabham, age 16

children out to work. Poverty is the cause of child labor, which causes further poverty and more children being employed to support their families. It is a vicious circle in which millions of Indians are trapped.

Inequalities in Society

Although India has become a wealthier country by industrializing, its wealth has not been shared equally between the cities and the countryside. Industries have developed around the cities, and it is here that the wealth they have generated has been spent. The countryside has not benefited. For example, the number of country people who can read and write is half the number of people living in the cities. In the villages, nearly twice as many babies die before their first birthdays as in the cities. There are more schools and better health care in the cities than in the countryside, and, as a result, there are more poor people and greater poverty in the countryside.

Only the richer city people can afford scooters for transportation.

We work harder to make up for the money lost by sending two children to school, but it's worth it. My wife and I have suffered because we can neither read nor write. We don't want our children to have the same problems.
—Jangaiah, farm laborer in Andhra Pradesh state

28

India is a nation of country people: nearly 75 percent of the population lives there, in 578,000 villages. The villagers' most important possession is land. It provides them with food for eating or selling. Cows can be grazed on it to supply milk and dung, which is both a fertilizer and a fuel. Land can be used as security to obtain a loan.

In India, the land is owned unequally: a few people own a lot of it and millions none. In between these two groups are the millions of subsistence farmers who own small plots. The British were partly responsible for this inequality in land ownership. They encouraged the *zamindars* to seize the land of the peasant farmers who could not pay their land tax. The *zamindars* ended up with huge areas of land, which their families still own. Today, it has been estimated that 3 percent of the population owns 40 percent of the land. Since Independence, laws have been made to redistribute the land more fairly. However, the laws have not been obeyed, and landless people have lacked the confidence to protest.

Most large landowners abuse their powerful positions in rural society. They rent land to landless people in return for a share of the harvests. Frequently, this is an unfair share, which leaves the farmers with only just enough for survival. Other landless people work as laborers for the large landowners, who pay them low wages.

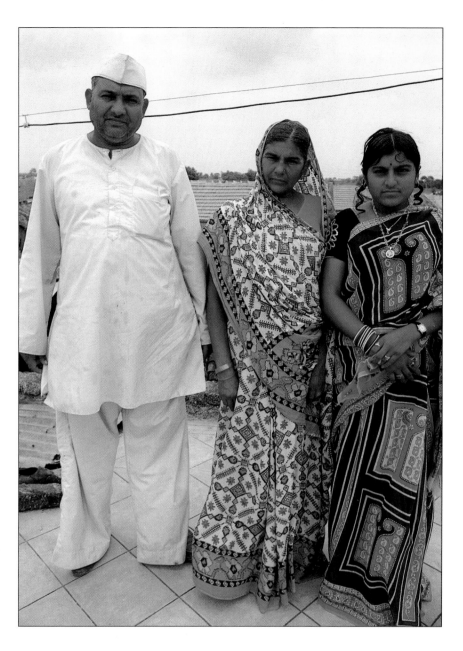

A rich landowner in Gujarat state. Many people who own land have grown wealthy by treating other people unjustly.

People come to the large landowners—who are the richest people in the country—to borrow money. They will be lent it on condition that it is repaid at a high interest rate. Many borrowers fall behind with their repayments and sink further into debt. It is not unusual for the debt to grow so big that it cannot be repaid in the borrower's lifetime, so it is passed on to his children. Whole families can end up in "bonded labor" to a moneylender, working solely for him until an inherited debt is paid off.

Country people can have difficult lives. If they have no land, they are in the power of greedy landowners. But even if they have their own land, they are still at the mercy of the monsoon. If the rains do not come, or flooding occurs, they may not have enough food. Often, the only way many people can survive is by borrowing from the moneylenders.

Country people try to improve their lives by having many children. In developed countries, large families are seen as a drain on income: the more children someone has, the more it will cost to feed, clothe, and educate them. Poor Indians take the opposite view: children can earn money to increase the family income. Many families now rely on their children for incomes. Children can also look after their parents in old age, something that is important in a country where pensions and old people's homes are rare. Because of the low quality of health care in villages, many children die young. In order to ensure that a few of them survive to adulthood, parents have many children.

Most country people think that large families are a help, not a hindrance. This potter's children can help him with his work so that he can earn more money.

TYPICAL MEALS EATEN BY COUNTRY PEOPLE
Breakfast:	In the north, *paratha* (thick pancake); in the south *idli* (rice dumpling), and a spicy sauce.
Lunch:	Rice, *dhal* (lentil soup), and vegetables, or, in the south, *masala dosa* (stuffed pancake).
Dinner:	Rice, vegetables, beans, and *chapatis* (thin pancakes).

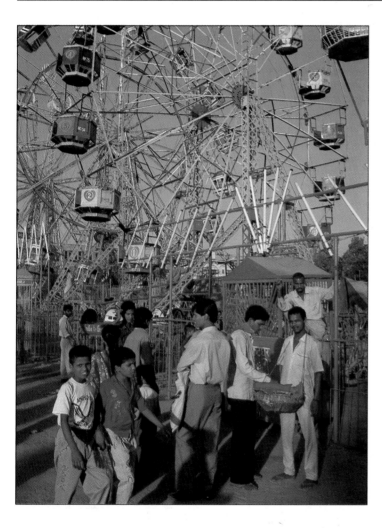

Opportunities for entertainment, as well as work, are more plentiful in cities than in the countryside.

While this may help individual families to survive, it worsens the situation for country people as a whole. Already, there are not enough resources for the existing people, so more people will mean that everyone is worse off. For example, farmland is the scarcest resource. The more children in a family, the smaller their share of land on their father's death. The smaller the land, the more difficult it is to grow enough to eat. In the end, a rapidly expanding population threatens the availability of land. It is a country person's most important possession; life is miserable without it.

As India's cities have developed, millions of country people have left the land and moved to them in the hope of having better, and easier, lives there.

CITY LIFE

City life rarely lives up to the hopes of most rural migrants. Once the rural poor, they are now part of the urban poor. They remain on the lowest rung of the social ladder. Even so, few of them regret their decisions to leave their villages, because they now have access to a wider range of facilities, from basic necessities to leisure activities, such as movies and parks. There are also more opportunities to earn income, especially for landless people. Previously, their jobs had been seasonal and affected by the weather. In the cities, the jobs are more regular, regardless of the climate.

31

There are not enough factory jobs for the thousands of rural people who arrive in the cities every day. Most of the migrants end up doing a variety of odd jobs. The industrialization of India has created a wealthy middle class of city businesspeople who require workers in their offices, factories, and homes. Employees, too, are needed by the new industries, stores, restaurants, and hotels opened to cater to the demands of this new class of people, many of whom have a lot of money to spend. Their incomes equal those of wealthy people in developed countries, and they aspire to a similar lifestyle, with designer-label clothes, expensive cars, foreign vacations, and all the latest household machines.

Educated and with good jobs, these two city women have lifestyles that country women can only dream about.

THE CASTE SYSTEM

Hindus are divided into four social groups, or castes:
- At the top are the Brahmins, from whom the priests are chosen.
- Next are the Kshatriyas, the soldiers and officials.
- Then come the Vaishyas, the business- and craftspeople.
- Finally, there are the Sudras, the farmers, servants, and laborers.

Separate from these castes—literally, "out-castes"—are the Untouchables, the people with the dirtiest jobs. Today, they prefer to call themselves Dalits, which means "the oppressed." They comprise 16 percent of the population.

Generally, people in the higher castes have the best opportunities in life. For example, 53 percent of all government officials are Brahmins, even though Brahmins make up only 3 percent of the population. In the countryside, the upper castes own most of the land, while the lower castes are more often landless.

In country villages, each caste often has its own neighborhood—with the Dalits living separately—and people marry only within their own castes. In many villages, if a Dalit were to drink from a Brahmin's well, he or she would be stoned to death.

Fueled by rural migration and the middle class's money, India's cities have exploded in size. Between 1971 and 1981, they grew by 45 percent; Bangalore alone rose by 77 percent. They have reached the bursting point. Public transportation groans under the weight of double the number of passengers it was designed to carry; power stations cannot cope with the increased demand for electricity, nor can sewage pipes deal with the greater amount of waste.

Although they are affected by the problems, the wealthy, urban middle class has the resources to cope with them. They have elegant homes, cars, servants, and generators for their air-conditioners. The urban poor have none of these, so they suffer the most. For example, there is a major shortage of housing in all the cities, which means that homes are very expensive. Unable to afford them, millions of poor people are forced to live on the streets and in shacks in dirty slums, where diseases spread rapidly in the hot climate. In 1990, the Indian government estimated that almost 49 million people lived in slums in India, the majority of them in the cities.

INDIAN MOVIES

India is the word's largest producer of movies. Each year, it produces three times as many movies as the United States.

A lack of housing means that many village people end up living in filthy city slums, like this one in Delhi.

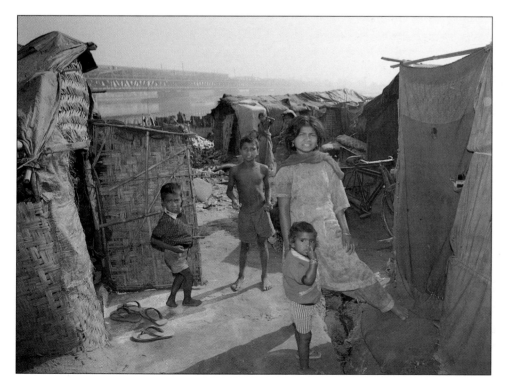

We thought that city life would be better. We've ended up in a shantytown on the banks of a stinking river full of garbage. We live in a hut made of pieces of wood and plastic we've found. It leaks in the rain. There's no electricity and no water, and the children always seem to be sick.
—Santosh Kumari, hotel porter in Delhi

The Indian government does not have the money to look after this deformed man, so he is forced to beg to survive.

SOCIAL INEQUALITIES

There are many divisions within Indian society that prevent people from improving their lives.

Caste is the biggest barrier to progress. It is very difficult for members of the lowest castes to get good educations and important jobs. By law, a percentage of university admissions and government jobs have to be given to low-caste people. However, putting this into practice has not been easy. Caste is less of a problem in the cities, but in the country it is still a handicap.

Before independence, Pakistan and Bangladesh were part of India. In 1947, it was decided that India would be a Hindu nation and that the areas where the Muslims lived would become separate Islamic countries. However, many Muslims continued to live in India. Although by law there is no religious discrimination, there is rivalry between the two religions, which often breaks out into violence, and Hindus tend to be given preference over Muslims.

India has traditionally been a male-dominated society. In the cities, there is now more equality between the sexes, but in the countryside the men still make all the important decisions.

RELIGIOUS GROUPS	
	Percentage of population
Hindus	82.6
Muslims	11.3
Christians	2.4
Sikhs	2.0
Buddhists	0.7
Jains	0.5
Others	0.5
Source: *India Book, 1994–95,* D. M. Silvera	

INEQUALITY BETWEEN THE SEXES

India is one of the few countries in the world where there are fewer women than men. Men are valued more than women because they have traditionally been the income earners, while women have stayed at home. Since women usually do not earn money, they are expected to bring some wealth with them when they marry. This is the reasoning behind paying a dowry: the bride's family presents her future husband with jewelry, furniture, clothes, and, if they are rich, a car or motorcycle. Even though dowry payments have been banned by law, many families still expect to receive them.

Parents, whether they are rich or poor, consider daughters a burden because dowry payments usually land them in heavy debt. Often, poor families will not look after a daughter properly, and so many girls die young. In the poorest regions of India, some families take more drastic action: they kill their daughters at birth. A booming business in the cities are clinics where a pregnant woman can discover the sex of her fetus. If it is female, it will be aborted.

MRS. INDIRA GANDHI

Indira Gandhi was the daughter of Jawaharlal Nehru, the first prime minister of Independent India. She also entered politics and became prime minister herself from 1966–77 and 1980–84. Although many of her policies were controversial, she was a strong leader who was devoted to national unity and to the reduction of poverty.

Despite the lowly status of many women, education, wealth, and a tough personality all helped Indira Gandhi (bottom right) *reach the top in politics.*

Girl killing is also traditional in parts of southern India, particularly in the poor Salem district of Tamil Nadu … 51 percent of families in Salem killed baby girls within a week of their birth to avoid dowry, currently running at around 60,000 rupees—the equivalent of 50 months' wages for an unskilled worker.

—*Source:* **The Times of India** *magazine, March 5, 1994*

Development: Improving People's Lives

Nongovernmental organizations (NGOs) are groups of people who have been helping India's poor since British times. The first NGOs were British missionaries and charity workers, who opened churches, schools, hospitals, and orphanages. While the poor benefited from their good works in their daily lives, these early NGOs could not halt the number of people who were becoming poor.

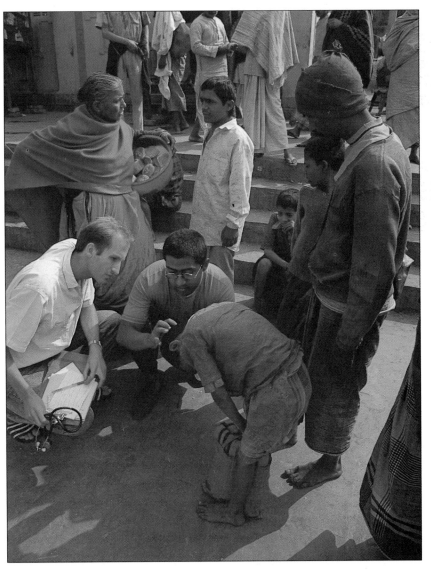

In the 1960s, the NGOs decided to adopt a different approach. They thought the solution lay in improving conditions by doing things like digging wells for irrigation and providing better health care. While this was an improvement on the earlier efforts, the poor were rarely consulted about what they wanted and little was done to end the social problems that caused poverty. A well may have cured a water problem in a village, but it did nothing to stop a powerful landowner from robbing the villagers of their land. The Indian people knew this was the real problem, but they had not been asked about it. A lot of money was wasted on unnecessary projects, and the poor continued to grow in numbers.

Providing clean water often helps people to live healthier lives, but the underlying causes of poverty are often more difficult to solve.

Today it is thought that the best way to tackle poverty is to ask people about their problems and let them suggest the best ways of solving them. Only in this way can people be helped to help themselves, so that in the future they will not need any outside assistance to lead better lives. This approach also tackles many of the social reasons behind long-term poverty.

Most NGOs in India have concentrated on working in the countryside, where poverty is at its worst. Raising the level of literacy is now considered to be one of the most important ways to improve people's lives. People without an education are open to all sorts of unjust treatment, which holds back their progress. Moneylenders, for example, can cheat them because they cannot read a loan agreement. Once people can read and write, they are more aware of their rights under the law, which gives them the confidence to challenge people who mistreat them.

Educated people, too, are open to new ideas. When mothers attend literacy classes, their children's health also improves, because the teachers often discuss such matters as child care, diet, and hygiene. Educated people can learn more easily how to take better care of their children. The chances of their children living to adulthood are much greater, thus reducing the need for such big families.

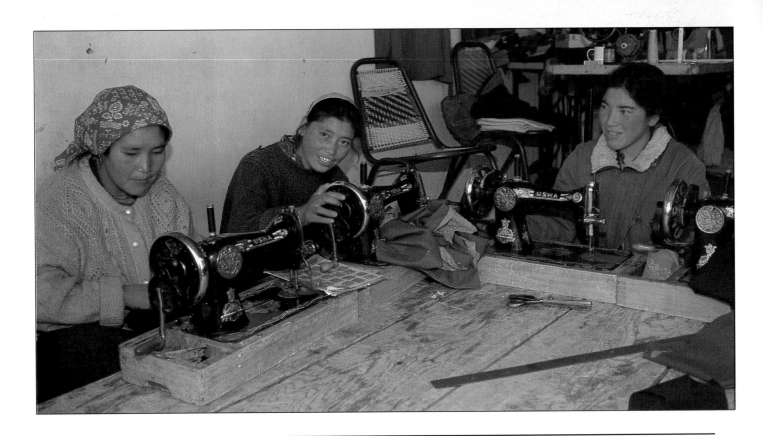

*Village women
being taught how
to use sewing
machines, so that
they can start their
own clothes
businesses*

*We are being trained to work sewing machines as part of a
plan to increase job opportunities for women. At the end of
the course, I can take a sewing machine back to my village.
There I will make clothes to sell, as well as train other women
to help me.*
—Dolma, from a mountain village in Ladakh

Although it is certainly a bonus, education on its own
cannot help landless people to earn a living. If, however,
they are taught a skill—perhaps a craft such as weaving or
carpentry—they may find regular, better-paid employment.
Alternatively, it may help to have money to start their own
businesses.

NGOs can help with special loans, at low interest rates, so
that a newly trained tailor, for example, can buy a sewing
machine without getting into high-interest debt with the
local moneylender. Farmers, too, can take advantage of these
loans to purchase things, such as high-yielding varieties of
seeds, fertilizers, and pesticides or to dig wells or irrigation
channels that will improve their ability to grow food.

DEVELOPMENT IN CHEMBAKOLLI

Chembakolli is a remote village among the forested hills in the southern state of Tamil Nadu. It is home to a community of Adivasis, people who are the descendants of the original inhabitants of India. The 51.5 million Adivasis are outcasts, like the Dalits, and live throughout central and southern India. They are mostly subsistence farmers. In Chembakolli, they grow rice, onions, tomatoes, peppers, and oranges for themselves, plus a little tea and coffee as cash crops.

Rejected by society, the Adivasis are illiterate, own little land, and have very limited access to health care and education. In the past, their communities have been badly organized, so they have been unable to prevent the government and rich landowners from taking away large areas of their land and cutting down the forests. Now, their future is under threat.

Since 1987, an Indian NGO, ACCORD, has been helping the people of Chembakolli to overcome their problems and to fight for their rights. ACCORD has been encouraging the villagers to act together, telling them that they have more power as a group than as individuals. At their regular community meetings, or *sanghams*, the villagers were soon listing all their problems, deciding how urgent each was and taking the appropriate action.

Chembakolli is located in the far south of India. The nearest town is 20 miles away, down rough dirt roads. Mysore, the closest city, is another 60 miles distant.

We know that any problem can be solved because we are a group, not just individuals. We are not afraid any more.
—Kelu, who regularly attends sanghams in Chembakolli

A sangham in Chembakolli, where people work out how to solve problems that affect them all.

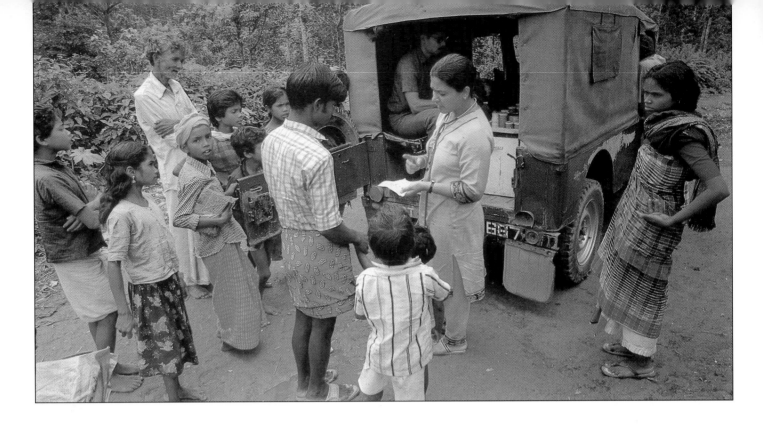

IMPROVING LIFE IN CHEMBAKOLLI

Before doctors visited Chembakolli regularly, people had to walk many miles if they needed medical help.

Money was an issue worrying many people, so ACCORD helped the villagers start a cooperative credit plan, into which everyone pays two rupees a month. The money is loaned out, for example, to pay off debts to landlords and moneylenders, to buy seeds, or to build a house. It is repaid at a very low rate of interest.

The credit plan is also used to pay two doctors to visit the village regularly. They treat the sick, as well as giving advice on staying healthy. They vaccinate children against polio and measles and hold classes on baby care for pregnant mothers. As a result, fewer babies are dying in their first year and children are living longer. The doctors have also trained health workers in Chembakolli to look after and advise the villagers between their visits.

Buying tea seedlings with the village credit scheme has allowed some people to increase the amount of money they earn.

The villagers realized that tea would be a good cash crop to earn extra money. However, they were short of money to buy the tea seedlings and confused about the ownership of suitable land. The village credit plan provided the money for the seedlings, and ACCORD assisted in deciding landownership matters.

Tea used to be the big man's crop. We knew it would be good to grow but we never had enough money for the seeds. Now that we have our own land and seeds we can plant in it.
—Karunakan, who now grows tea on his land

ACCORD has also helped to open a school in Chembakolli. Previously, Adivasi children had gone to local government schools, which they did not like. The children felt very inferior to their upper-caste classmates. The new school is run by villagers who have been trained as teachers by ACCORD. They understand that education is not just about reading, writing, and arithmetic: it must make the Adivasi children proud of their culture and confident in their dealings with other Indians, whether Dalits or Brahmins. The teachers also emphasize the need to take care of the environment, for as it deteriorates so do the Adivasis' chances of better lives.

Adivasi children find it easier to learn at their own school.

When I was a child, I went to a government school. There was only one other Adivasi child there. We used to wear gold earrings, which the other children made fun of. They couldn't understand our language. The teacher told us not to speak it in school but didn't tell us why. For 12 years I felt that everyone was superior to me.
—Penchi, who sends his children to the new school

STREET CHILDREN

All of India's street children miss out on education. Living on the streets also affects their health, both physically and mentally. They do not grow as tall as other children because they have poor diets, sometimes eating food from garbage cans. Long after others have grown up, street children are still behaving like children half their age.

Working Toward a Brighter Future

In Bangalore, several NGOs are helping street children to get a better start in life. These NGOs have opened shelters that are home for some children, while others just visit them during the day. They are also helping the children by teaching them skills that will allow them to get jobs. Some shelters give the children food, health advice, and classes in carpentry, screen printing, tailoring, and electronics.

On the streets my biggest problem was food; also the police used to arrest me and I had to pay them money to get away. Now I'm in [a] shelter and I wear decent clothes, and eat and wash every day. My lessons are also helping me to start planning for the future. None of this would have happened a few years ago.
—Bijl, age 10

Bijl, on the left, now has hope for a better future since he began going to the shelter.

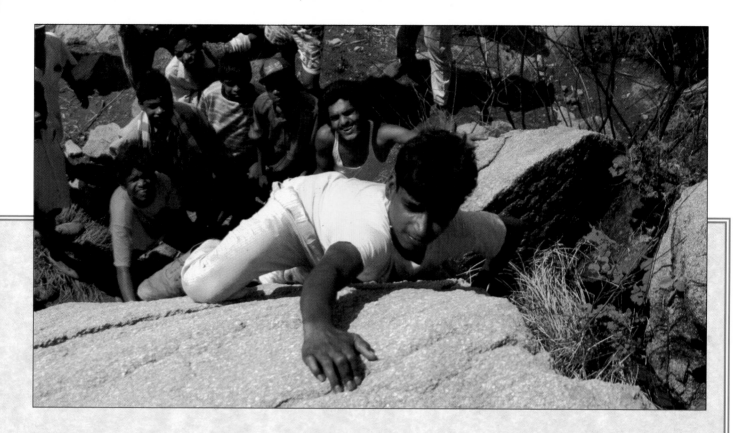

Outdoor pursuits also help to give the shelter's children the confidence to cope with challenging situations.

Children over 16 can go to another NGO after they have learned a skill. The staff tries to find them jobs with local firms, most of whom are usually reluctant to employ ex-street children. To make it easier for them to get employed, the teenagers are

Local employers want responsible, reliable, honest workers—qualities they don't think street children have. My job is to convince them that they're wrong. You can find these qualities in our teenagers.
—Solomon Jayaprakash, who works in a shelter

I've been working as a garage mechanic for one year. It's a great job and I would like to open my own business one day. Without help, I'd still be a rag picker, and I never want to go back to that.
—Lokech, one of the shelters' success stories

taught the skills they need to keep full-time jobs. There is also an effort to build up their self-confidence with outdoor activities, such as rock climbing, that encourage them to tackle difficult tasks.

India Tomorrow

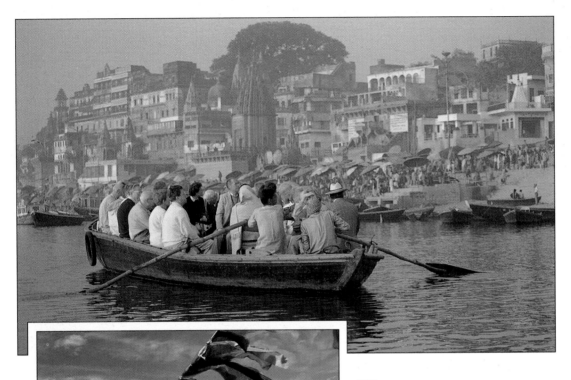

Many tourists visit India. The money they bring into the country is an important source of income.

Cut off by the high Himalayas, Ladakh has missed out on India's post-independence prosperity.

There is no doubt that India has made a great leap forward after independence. In 1947, only 15 percent of adults could read and write; few could expect to live beyond their late twenties; there were frequent food shortages; hardly any villages had electricity; and there was very little industry. Even so, despite the progress, today India has twice as many poor people as neighboring China, which has a bigger population.

Mahatma Gandhi believed that poverty could be reduced if India concentrated on improving conditions in the countryside. As the countryside prospered, Gandhi said, it would push the rest of India forward: India would develop from the bottom up.

Jawaharlal Nehru, independent India's first prime minister, believed the opposite: India should advance from the top down. Nehru gave priority to heavy industries in the belief that they would pull India forward, with all Indians benefiting from the progress.

It is hoped that the wealth created by India's new industries will trickle down to these street sellers.

Today, the government continues to follow Nehru's line of thinking. It considers that the wealth created by the rich people at the top will trickle down to the poor below them. The government anticipates that the richer the middle class becomes, the more it will buy. Then, more factories will have to be built, and more jobs will become available for the poor. If this happens, all India's people will be better off.

Even if this plan works, it may be many years before there are any noticeable benefits. Until then, India's poor will need to be supported so that they are in better positions to improve their own lives.

FOREIGN DEBT

To help pay for India's industrialization, the government has had to borrow money. In 1992, the World Bank said India owed a total of $72 billion, which will rise to $92 billion by 1997. Every year, India has to use 13 percent of its earnings from exports to repay this debt. The further into debt India gets, the more difficult it is for India to help its own people.

Source: *World Development Report*, World Bank, 1994

Glossary

Alluvium Earth or sand left behind by flood or river waters.

Astronomy Study of the sun, moon, planets, and stars.

Calorie A unit of energy produced by food.

Census A government count of all the people in a country.

Colonialism The control of a country by another country that is usually richer and more powerful. The controlled country becomes a colony.

Deforestation Cutting down large areas of forest.

Debt Owing money to another person or country.

Dependent Someone, such as a child, who depends on another person to earn money and for support.

Famine Exists when there is not enough food for everyone.

Fertilizer Something added to the soil to make it better for growing crops.

Gross National Product (GNP) The money a country earns within its borders, plus money from exports.

Illiterate Being unable to read or write.

Independence Occurs when a colony becomes free from foreign rule.

Indigo A blue dye, for dying cloth such as cotton, obtained from a plant.

Interest rate The money that has to be repaid regularly to pay for money that has been borrowed.

Irrigation Adding water to land that would be too dry otherwise to grow crops.

Jute A fiber obtained from the bark of a plant, used to make sacks and mats.

Life expectancy The number of years a person can expect to live.

Literacy Being able to read and write.

Loan Money that has been borrowed.

Malnourished Not having enough food to eat.

Migrant A person who has moved from home to live in another town or country.

Monsoon The name of the wind that brings the summer rain; the rainy season, too, is often referred to as the monsoon.

Overgrazing Allowing animals on pasture to eat too much, so that the land becomes bare. This often leads to soil erosion.

Pesticides Chemicals used to kill insects to stop them from eating and destroying crops.

Raw materials Materials in their natural state, such as coal and iron ore.

Recycling Turning trash and waste into something that can be reused.

Sanitation Drains and pipes for removing waste.

Service industries Industries, such as tourism and banking, that do not make goods but supply people with services they need.

Soil erosion The wearing away of the soil by wind or rain.

Subsistence Growing food or earning money that is just enough to live on.

Tourist Person from a different country who is visiting.

Zamindars Large landowners who became powerful under British rule.

Further Information

Addresses

India Tourist Office, 30 Rockefeller Plaza North, New York, NY 10112 will provide general information on India.

State of the World's Children is an annual report with information on developing countries, available from UNICEF, 1 UN Plaza, New York, NY 10017.

OXFAM America, 115 Broadway, Boston, MA 02116 will provide information on small-scale development projects in India.

Books

Ashton, Stephen. *The British in India.* North Pomfret, VT: Trafalgar Square, 1988.

Cumming, David. *The Ganges.* Rivers of the World. Milwaukee: Raintree Steck-Vaughn, 1993.

Hull, Robert. *Indian Stories.* Tales from Around the World. New York: Thomson Learning, 1994.

India in Pictures. Revised edition. Visual Geography. Minneapolis: Lerner Publications, 1992.

Kadodwala, Dilip. *Hinduism.* World Religions. New York: Thomson Learning, 1995.

Kaur, Sharon. *Food in India.* International Food Library. Vero Beach, FL: Rourke Corp., 1989.

Bush, Catherine. *Mohandas K. Gandhi.* World Leaders—Past and Present. New York: Chelsea House, 1985.

Warner, Rachel. *Indian Migrations.* Migrations. New York: Thomson Learning, 1995.

Films

Gandhi (1982) A dramatization of the life of India's most famous leader. Winner of eight Academy Awards.

Heat and Dust (1982) Contrasting stories of a woman living in 1920s colonial India, and her great-niece who arrives there 60 years later.

The Jewel in the Crown (1984) Rich drama about the last years of English rule in India. Originally shown on television in 14 episodes.

Salaam Bombay! (1988) A realistic portrayal of street children in Bombay.

Index

Numbers in **bold** refer to illustrations

48